Garage

FUNNY CARS

DEANNA CASWELL

WORLD BOOK

This World Book edition of *Funny Cars*
is published by agreement between
Black Rabbit Books and World Book, Inc.
© 2018 Black Rabbit Books,
2140 Howard Dr. West,
North Mankato, MN 56003 U.S.A.
World Book, Inc.,
180 North LaSalle St., Suite 900,
Chicago, IL 60601 U.S.A.

Jennifer Besel, editor; Grant Gould, interior designer; Michael Sellner,
cover designer; Omay Ayres, photo researcher

Library of Congress Control Number: 2016050035

ISBN: 978-0-7166-9304-8

Printed in the United States at CG Book Printers,
North Mankato, Minnesota, 56003. 3/17

Image Credits
Alamy: Leo Mason sports pho-
tos, 8; Tony Watson, 20–21; Volodymyr
Horbovyy, 14–15 (flag); ZUMA Press, Inc,
26; Dreamstime: Walter Arce, 8–9; Getty Imag-
es: Alvis Upitis, 29 (top); The Enthusiast Network,
10; Newscom: Bizuayehu Tesfaye/Icon Sportswire
DHU, 6–7; David Allio, 4–5; David Allio/Icon SMI
951, 23; David Allio/Icon Sportswire 951, 22; David
Griffin/Icon SMI 953, 3; David J. Griffin/Icon SMI
953, 32; Duncan Williams, 12–13, 24–25; Jeff Speer/
Icon Sportswire CEO, 16; Shutterstock: Action Sports
Photography, Front Cover, Back Cover, 1, 19 (car), 31;
Castleski, 28; Ken Tannenbaum, 29 (bottom); Iaroslav
Neliubov, 17; mamanamsai, 19 (speedometer);
Philip Pilosian, 28–29 (car)
Every effort has been made to contact copyright
holders for material reproduced in this
book. Any omissions will be rectified
in subsequent printings if notice is
given to the publisher.

CONTENTS

CHAPTER 1

Fast and Fun

The driver gets his Funny Car (FC) ready for the race. He warms up the car by spinning its wheels down the track. The car roars. Smoke fills the air.

Then the driver backs up to the start line. The light turns green, and the car blasts away. Four seconds later, two parachutes pop open. The sudden braking slams the driver's body forward.

Burning Up the Track

Funny Cars are used in **drag races**. They are built for speed. They look almost like everyday cars. But they don't run like regular cars.

FCs go the length of more than four football fields in about five seconds.

FCs are slim and have high back ends. They use parachutes to stop. And they go fast.

By the Numbers

$300,000
COST TO BUILD AN FC

.8 SECOND
time it takes an FC to
go from 0 to 100 miles
(161 kilometers) per hour

about 2,575 pounds
(1,168 kilograms)

WEIGHT OF AN FC WITH DRIVER

time of an **FC race**

ABOUT **5** SECONDS

FC race length **1,000 feet** (305 meters)

Moving the wheels forward made the cars look odd. People called them "funny cars." The name stuck.

CHAPTER 2

The History of Funny Cars

In the 1950s and 1960s, drag racing became popular. In 1964, Jack Chrisman used a dragster that ran on **nitromethane**. The car was too powerful for its tires. The tires spun and smoked the length of the track. Fans went wild. A new kind of racing was born.

The next year, a team made a change to these nitro cars. They moved the front and back wheels forward. The cars held to the road better.

Flip-Tops

Drag-racing rules said FCs had to look like regular cars. But regular cars are heavy. In 1966, one company had a great idea. It put a regular car body over a lightweight dragster **frame**. The doors and hood didn't open. The whole body flipped up.

WHERE FUNNY CARS RACE

Today, FCs race in almost every U.S. state.
Many other countries have FC races too.

UNITED KINGDOM

ICELAND

CANADA

UNITED STATES

NETHERLANDS

PUERTO RICO

NORWAY

FINLAND

SWEDEN

GERMANY

HUNGARY

ITALY

AUSTRALIA

NEW ZEALAND

CHAPTER 3

Built for Speed

FCs run on nitromethane. Nitro is a stronger fuel than gas. It gives FC engines more power. FCs use V-8 engines to speed down tracks.

FCs use up to five gallons (19 liters) of fuel in a .25-mile (.4-km) race.

Shape and Wind

Car bodies that cut through the air go faster. Today's FCs have skinny bodies. These bodies help the cars go record speeds.

National Hot Rod Association
Speed Records

COMPARING
TOP SPEEDS

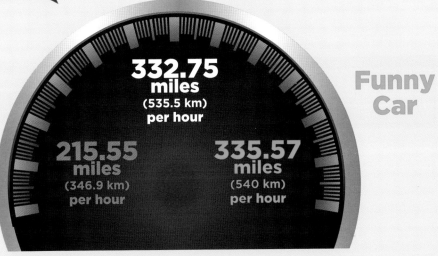

Top Fuel Dragster

Pro Stock Car

Funny Car

332.75 miles
(535.5 km)
per hour

215.55 miles
(346.9 km)
per hour

335.57 miles
(540 km)
per hour

(THROUGH 2016)

FUNNY CAR PARTS

GREENHOUSE

SUPERCHARGER

FUEL TANK

ENGINE

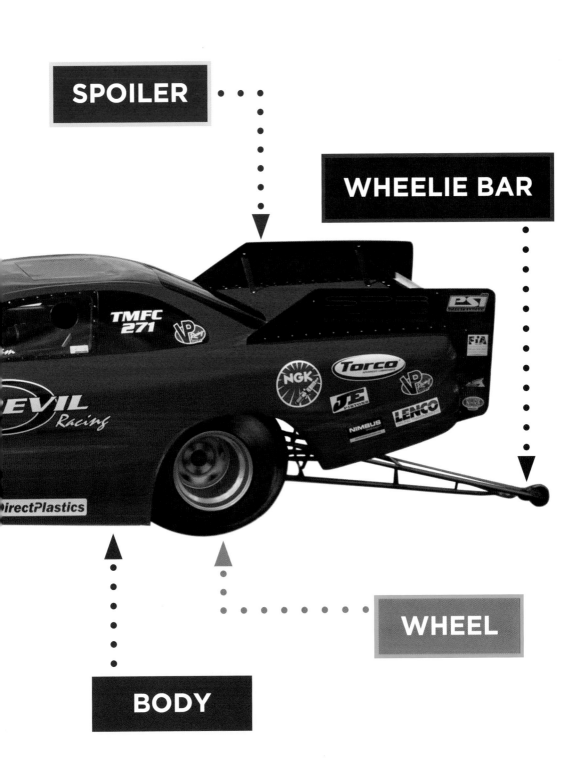

SPOILER

WHEELIE BAR

WHEEL

BODY

JOHN FORCE

Most Career Funny Car Wins
in the National Hot Rod Association
(through 2016)

	wins
John Force	
Ron Capps	49
Tony Pedregon	43
Robert Hight	37
Don Prudhomme	35

wins   20   40

Great Drivers

FCs are powerful. But it takes more than power to win. An FC race is only about five seconds long. And FCs are hard to control. Drivers have to think fast. Slow **reactions** lose races.

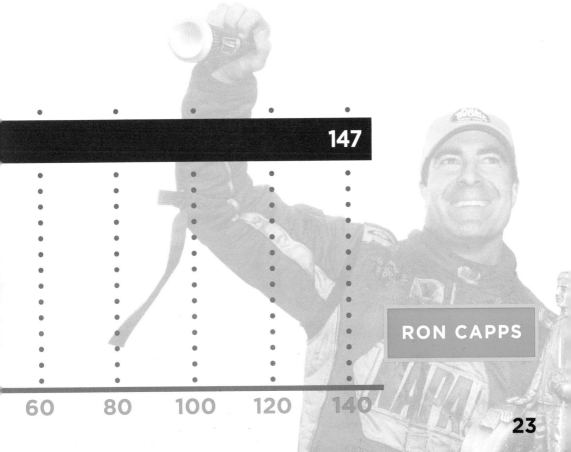

147

RON CAPPS

60   80   100   120   140

CHAPTER 4

The Future of Funny Cars

Today, FCs have more power and better **grip** than ever before. They reach speeds above 330 miles (531 km) per hour. New technology will play a role in future FCs. Maybe designers will use 3-D printing to create new parts.

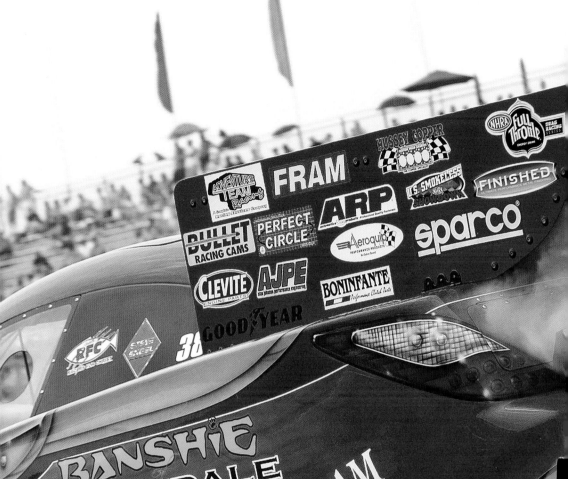

Funnier Year by Year

Over the years, FCs have gotten lighter, stronger, and faster. No one knows what future FCs will look like. But one thing won't change. These cars will always be

fast and fun.

The 2015 Dodge Charger shell uses bulletproof material. This material is light but still very strong.

1964

Jack Chrisman introduces first nitro car.

1965

Funny Cars get their name.

1945

World War II ends.

1945

The first people walk on the moon.

1969

1984

Kenny Bernstein introduces an FC with a new body design. His car slices through the air.

2013

John Force wins 16th championship.

2016

The Mount St. Helens volcano erupts.

1980

Terrorists attack the World Trade Center and Pentagon.

2001

drag race (DRAYG RAYS)—a contest where people race cars at very high speeds over a short distance

frame (FRAYM)—the structure that supports the body of a motorcycle or automobile

greenhouse (GREEN-hauws)—a shell that covers the section of a Funny Car where the driver sits

grip (GRIP)—the ability to hold firmly

nitromethane (ny-tro-MEH-thayn)—a liquid fuel for high-performance engines and rockets

reaction (ree-AK-shun)—the way someone acts or feels in response to something that happens

supercharger (SOO-pur-char-jur)—a device that brings in more air to an engine

BOOKS

Caswell, Deanna. *Top Fuel Dragsters.* Gearhead Garage. North Mankato, MN: Black Rabbit Books, 2018.

Gigliotti, Jim. *Smokin' Dragsters and Funny Cars.* Fast Wheels! Berkeley Heights, NJ: Enslow Publishers, Inc., 2013.

MacArthur, Collin. *Inside a Drag Racer.* Life in the Fast Lane. New York: Cavendish Square, 2015.

WEBSITES

AMSOIL Nitro Funny Car Drivers
www.ihradrs.com/drivers/amsoil-nitro-funny-cars/

Basics of Drag Racing
www.nhra.com/nhra101/basics.aspx

Drag Racing Classes
www.nhra.com/nhra101/classes.aspx

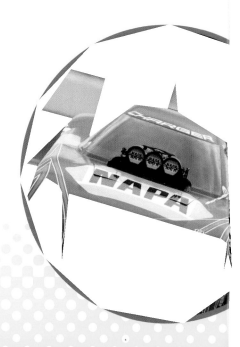